COLORFUL MINDS

TIPS FOR MANAGING YOUR EMOTIONS

The White Book

What to Do When You're Stressed

by
John Wood

BEARPORT
PUBLISHING

Minneapolis, Minnesota

Credits

Cover and throughout – Ekaterina Kapranova, Beatriz Gascon J. 4 – NLshop. 10 – gilaxia/iStock. 11 – rinrin_gs, Jason Erickson/iStock. 13 – Ekaterina Kapranova, Igor Levin, S-Victoria, Lubenica, iuliia_n, SashaShuArt, love pattern, carlosalvarez/iStock. 8-10 – jsabirova. 14 – olllikeballoon, hidesy/iStock. 15 – Alenka Karabanova. 18 – Mongta Studio/Shutterstock. 21 – Erstudiostok/iStock. 22 – NLshop. Additional illustrations by Danielle Webster-Jones. All images courtesy of Shutterstock.com. With thanks to Getty Images, Thinkstock Photo, and iStockphoto.

Library of Congress Cataloging-in-Publication Data is available at www.loc.gov or upon request from the publisher.

ISBN: 978-1-63691-873-0 (hardcover)
ISBN: 978-1-63691-881-5 (paperback)
ISBN: 978-1-63691-889-1 (ebook)

© 2023 Booklife Publishing

This edition is published by arrangement with Booklife Publishing.

North American adaptations © 2023 Bearport Publishing Company. All rights reserved. No part of this publication may be reproduced in whole or in part, stored in any retrieval system, or transmitted in any form or by any means, electronic, mechanical, photocopying, recording, or otherwise, without written permission from the publisher.

For more information, write to Bearport Publishing, 5357 Penn Avenue South, Minneapolis, MN 55419. Printed in the United States of America.

For more The White Book activities:

1. Go to **www.factsurfer.com**
2. Enter "**White Book**" into the search box.
3. Click on the cover of this book to see a list of activities.

CONTENTS

Imagine a Rainbow 4
The Relaxation Room 6
Animal Breath 8
Get Moving! 10
A B See 12
Dump That Stress! 14
Me Time 16
Super You 18
Little Ideas 20
Feeling Better? 22
Glossary 24
Index 24

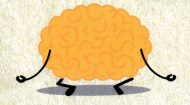

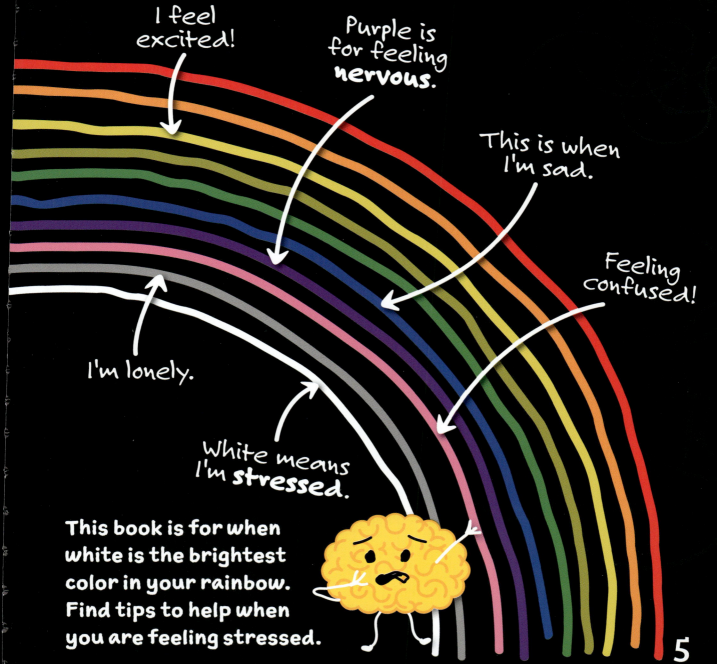

THE RELAXATION ROOM

When we are stressed, we are very worried that something will go wrong. But most of the time, everything turns out okay!

We can be less stressed and more **relaxed** if we **imagine** things going well instead.

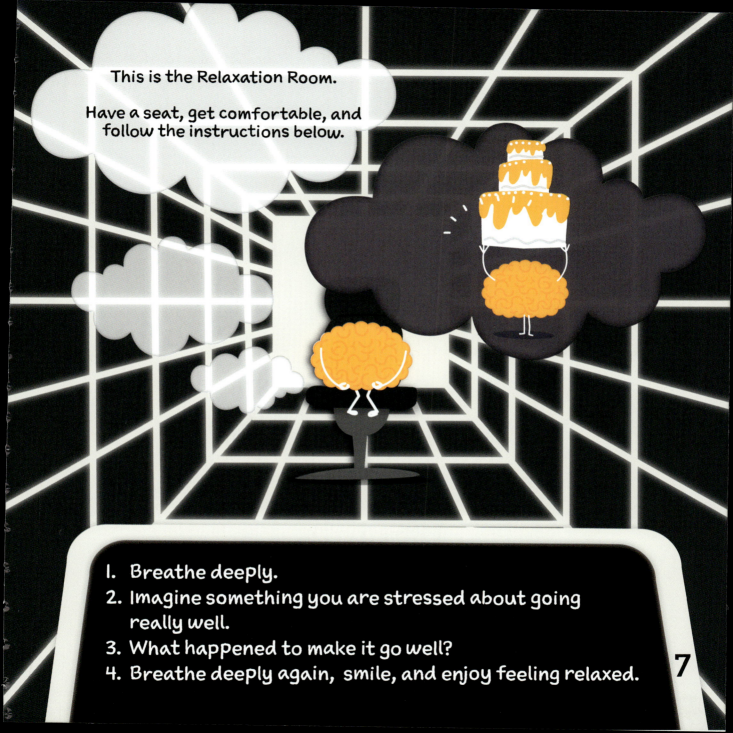

ANIMAL BREATH

When we feel stressed, we can start breathing very fast. This makes us feel even more stressed. If we take slow, deep breaths, it can calm us down.

Let's find a way to breathe in a fun but calming way. First, pick an animal.

Breathe in while counting to four in your head. Then, hold your breath for three seconds. After that, slowly breathe out while making the sound of your chosen animal.

GET → MOVING!

We might not feel like **exercising** when we are stressed, but it can make us feel much better. Any exercise is good, even a short walk!

TOP TIP!

The important thing is to move your body in a way that is fun for you and feels good!

Let's exercise! Move one space at a time and follow the instruction on each square. Or add any other movement that you like.

A B SEE

When we are stressed, it can be hard to think clearly.

One way we can stop stress from taking over our brains is to think only about what is around us.

The page to the right has objects that begins with each letter of the alphabet. Can you find all 26 objects? Do you feel calmer now?

DUMP THAT STRESS!

> Draw a picture of everything you are stressed about. If you are not sure what's making you stressed, your picture could just be a scribble of different colors!

When your drawing is finished, crumple it up. Then, throw it into a **recycling** bin and imagine you are throwing away the stressful thoughts, too.

WHAT DID YOU DRAW?

Lots of angry scribbled lines?

A person?

Lots of short, nervous little dashes?

Homework?

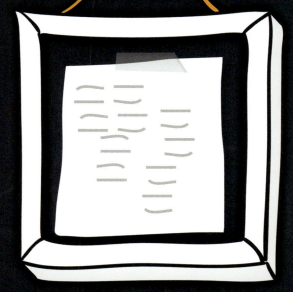

15

ME TIME

Doing too much stuff can cause stress! It can be really helpful to have me time. This means time where you can do what you want.

To the right is a **message** that tells people you are stressed and need time to yourself. Just show this message to an adult and then take some time to do something relaxing.

TOP TIP!

Some people like being busy and some people don't. There is no right or wrong!

Hello,

The child who showed you this page is feeling stressed. They might feel like talking later. But for now, they don't feel like they can answer any questions. They need some me time alone to do something relaxing. If you can help them do that, they will be very thankful!

SUPER YOU

Sometimes we can't control our stress. We might cry, slam the door, or shout at other people. When we've calmed down, we might feel silly. That is okay!

> When we feel like this, it is important to remember how super we are!

Grab a trusted adult or friend and follow the steps on the next page together.

STEP 1:
Grab some pencils and paper.

STEP 2:
Write something you are good at or why people like you. Don't let the other person see!

STEP 3:
Now, ask the other person to do the same thing about you.

STEP 4:
When you are both finished, show each other what makes you so super!

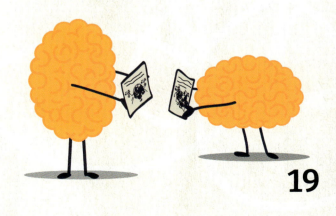

LITTLE IDEAS

There are lots of little tips and tricks we can use when we feel stressed.

SLEEP WELL

Getting good sleep can help you feel more relaxed.

EAT WELL

We can get stressed if we are not eating well. Try to make fruits and vegetables part of your **diet**.

REACH OUT

Make a list of adults you trust. If you get too stressed, you know who to go to for help.

COUNT ON IT

If something makes you stressed, count to ten before you do or say anything. This will stop you from doing something that you don't really mean.

FEELING BETTER?

Which tip worked best for you? Why do you think that is?

If you feel better, now is a good time to think about what made you feel stressed and why. How might you handle things the next time you feel stressed?

Remember, you are like everyone else. We all have colorful minds.

Every feeling you have is important! This book will still be here

whenever

you need it.

23

GLOSSARY

confident believing in one's abilities

diet the food that a person usually eats

exercising moving your body around to make it stronger and healthier

imagine to use your mind to make up something

message an idea or thought that one person sends or gives to someone else

nervous worried or afraid about what might happen

recycling turning old things, such as newspapers, metal cans, and glass bottles, into new things

relaxed feeling rested and enjoying yourself

stressed feeling very worried, especially about things not working out well

INDEX

breathing 7-9, 11
calming down 8-9, 12, 18
counting 9, 21
drawing 14-15
eating 20

exercise 10-11
imagining 6-7, 14
relaxation 6-7, 16-17, 20
sleeping 20
writing 19